AUNTIE BILLIE'S GREATEST INVENTION

Judy Allen has written more than fifty books –
fiction and non-fiction, for adults and children.
Her stories for children include *The Most Brilliant
Trick Ever*, *The Dim Thin Ducks*, *The Great Pig
Sprint*, *Seven Weird Days at Number 31*, *The
Dream Thing*, *Something Rare and Special*,
Travelling Hopefully and *Awaiting Developments*,
which won the Whitbread Award and the Friends
of the Earth Earthworm Award. She has a partic-
ular interest in ecological issues and is the author
of six Animals at Risk books – *Tiger*, *Panda*,
Whale, *Elephant*, *Eagle* and *Seal* – and the com-
piler of *Anthology for the Earth*.

Cavan
Wit

D0431674

Books by the same author

The Dim Thin Ducks

The Great Pig Sprint

What Is a Wall, After All?

The Most Brilliant Trick Ever

Seven Weird Days at Number 31

For older readers

Awaiting Developments

The Dream Thing

Something Rare and Special

Travelling Hopefully

JUDY ALLEN

Auntie Billie's GREATEST INVENTION

Illustrations by Chris Mould

WALKER BOOKS
AND SUBSIDIARIES
LONDON • BOSTON • SYDNEY

For Will

CAVAN COUNTY LIBRARY
ACC No. C 103182
CLASS NO. J 5-8
INVOICE NO 4562 Laburnum
PRICE £1·75

First published 1997 by
Walker Books Ltd, 87 Vauxhall Walk
London SE11 5HJ

This edition published 1998

2 4 6 8 10 9 7 5 3

Text © 1997 Judy Allen
Illustrations © 1997 Chris Mould

This book has been typeset in Garamond.

Printed in England by Clays Ltd, St Ives plc

British Library Cataloguing in Publication Data
A catalogue record for this book
is available from the British Library.

ISBN 0-7445-6011-X

Contents

The Mystery of the Shed

Dan and Ally enjoyed visiting their
Uncle Pat and Auntie Billie. They
liked Uncle Pat. He was an
excellent cook. They liked Auntie
Billie. *She* was an inventor.

Auntie Billie's inventions were brilliant ... even though they never lasted very long.

There was the Yuk-Digester, which crouched on the table at mealtimes and swallowed all the bones and stones and fruit-peel.

It worked very well. Too well. One day it swallowed so much it exploded.

There was the Muk-Shifter, which
went around the house searching
out crumbs and fluff and sticky bits
and throwing them away.

It worked very well. Too well.

One day it found a melted
chocolate bar behind the cooker
and got itself in such a mess it threw
itself away and was never seen
again.

Then there was the Flying-Space-Camera, which was designed to go on a round-trip to the moon to take photographs of the other side.

No one knew how well that worked because it hadn't come back yet.

Auntie Billie spent most of her time in her garden shed. That was where she did all her inventing and no one else was allowed in.

Whenever Dan and Ally arrived, she would come out, usually with something new to show them.

One day, though, she didn't come out of her shed. She stayed inside.

"She's busy with her Greatest Invention," said Uncle Pat. "It's at a very important stage. If you've nothing to do, you can come and work in my vegetable patch."

"It's all right, thank you," said Dan and Ally hastily. "We can find things to do."

An hour went by, then two, then three. Still Auntie Billie hadn't come out of her shed.

At last, when their aunt had missed two meals, including Uncle Pat's Perfect Pasta with Special Savoury Sauce and his Luscious Chocolate Mousse with Crispy Toffee-Chips, the children couldn't wait any longer.

As soon as Uncle Pat fell asleep in front of the television, they went out to the garden shed.

The window was too high to see through, the door was shut, and there was a sign hanging on a nail which said:

PRIVATE SECRET
KEEP OUT

They knocked on the door until
the KEEP OUT sign swung on its
nail.

They called until the dog next
door began to bark.

Finally, Dan crouched down so
Ally could stand on his back and
look in through the high window.

"What can you see?" said Dan.

"All kinds of stuff," said Ally.
"But I can't see Auntie Billie. She
isn't in there. She's disappeared."

Strange Changes

"The shed door hasn't got a lock," said Ally thoughtfully.

"But it has got a KEEP OUT sign," said Dan.

"I'm going in anyway," said Ally.

Dan knew he couldn't stop her so he followed her.

Not far inside the door, they almost trod on two things lying on the floor.

One was a piece of tree bark with something sticky leaking out of it. The other was a peculiarly shaped metal object.

Further into the shed there were
lots of other things. There was a
messy desk. There was a stool with
a cushion. There was a battered old
table, an armchair, a crate full of
files and papers, a box of tools and
instruments, and a plant in a pot.

Somehow, though, the peculiarly shaped metal object on the floor seemed the most interesting. It had a nozzle, a lever and a trigger. It looked very new and shiny.

Dan stared at it. "I bet that's her Greatest Invention," he said. "It looks like some kind of spray."

Ally picked it up and aimed at the old battered table. "Let's see what it does," she said.

"We shouldn't touch it!" said Dan, but too late. Ally had pulled the trigger. Nothing seemed to come out of the nozzle ... no liquid, no air, no sound. "It doesn't do anything," said Ally.

"Oh yes it does!" said Dan. "Look at the table."

The battered old table had changed completely. The scratches and marks had gone. It looked shiny and new.

"That's clever," said Ally. "She's invented an instant polish. I wonder if it will clean the window."

She aimed the spray
and pulled the
trigger again.

The dirty glass of
the window
became a fuzzy blur.
Then it disappeared.
A mug that had been standing on
the window-sill disappeared too.
There was nothing left
but a pile of dust.

"Oh no!" said
Ally. "It doesn't
clean things, it
destroys them!"

She dropped
the spray.

Dan picked it up. "That's odd," he said. "It didn't destroy the table."

He pointed it at the shiny table and pressed the trigger.

The table became a fuzzy blur. Then it vanished and in its place was a bit of tree.

Dan dropped the spray, too.

Ally picked it up again. "We fired too hard," she said. She aimed at the bamboo armchair. "I'll try a short squirt."

One moment there was an armchair, with a crate full of files and papers on the floor in front of it.

The next moment the chair had turned into a patch of tall grasses, with thick stems. The crate of papers was nowhere to be seen, but underneath the grasses was a greenish puddle with wood shavings in it. It smelled horrible.

"What *is* this thing?" said Ally. "What *has* she invented?"

"I think I know," said Dan. "Can't you guess?"

The Incredible Spray

"It's a time-spray," said Dan.

He scraped up some sand from the window-sill. "See?" he said. "Glass is made from sand."

He scraped up some earth in the other hand. "And the mug was made of clay," he said. "Clay comes from earth. The time-spray sent the

window glass and the mug back to
before they were made!"

"You mean the table's gone back
to when it was a bit of tree?" said
Ally.

"Exactly."

"So the chair was made of bamboo?" said Ally excitedly. "That's what that grass is?"

"Absolutely," said Dan importantly. "And the crate with the papers in it was plastic. Plastic comes from petroleum. That's what that puddle is."

"And there's the woodpulp the papers were made from, floating in the puddle!" said Ally.

Dan pointed the spray at the plant on the desk. "Watch it go back in time," he said.

The plant grew smaller and smaller. The plastic pot melted away. The earth fell out. The plant went on shrinking until it was only a seed. Then the seed vanished.

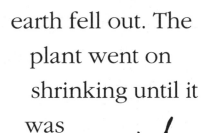

"There!" said Dan. "I've sent it back to a time before it existed."

"Let me try it on something else," said Ally, grabbing for the spray.

"Be careful!" said Dan, hanging on to it. "Don't point it at me."

They struggled and, in the confusion, the time-spray went off accidentally.

"Oops," said Ally.

Luckily the spray wasn't pointing at Dan. It was pointing at the cushion on the stool by the desk.

Instantly, the cushion disappeared. Where it had been there were several bits of white tufty stuff ... and one enormous duck.

"The cushion must have been made of cotton," said Dan, "and stuffed with duck feathers!"

Ally launched herself into a flying tackle and caught the duck as it was flapping out of the door.

"I've thought of something really worrying," said Dan.

"What?" said Ally, comforting the duck.

"Maybe Auntie Billie had an accident, too," said Dan. "Maybe she sent herself into the past by mistake!"

Time for an Experiment

"That's awful!" said Ally. "How can we get her back?"

"Perhaps if we switch that lever the other way," said Dan, "it might make things travel forwards in time instead of backwards."

"I can't do anything," said Ally. "I'm holding this duck."

Dan took a conker out
of his pocket and put
it on the floor. Then
he switched the lever,
took aim and fired.

The skin
of the conker split.
Roots came out of
the bottom. A sprout
came out of the top.
The roots
found their way
through a hole in
the floorboards.
The sprout grew
taller and thicker
and put out branches.

"Stop!" yelled Ally.
"The trigger's
stuck!" shouted
Dan, struggling
with it.
The
sprout
became a sapling.
The sapling became
a small tree. The
trunk
thickened, the
roots spread under
the floor, the
branches grew
longer, leaves and
flowers opened.

The shed creaked, groaned, and split its sides.

By the time Dan had managed to unstick the trigger, the shed had collapsed. In its place stood a large chestnut tree. Ally and the duck were sitting on one of its branches.

Dan stood on
the ground, beside
the bamboo and
the box of tools and
instruments, and
looked up at them.
"Perhaps we should
have obeyed that
KEEP OUT sign,"
he said.

Here and Now

Ally passed the duck to Dan and climbed down the tree. "At least we know how to bring Auntie Billie back," she said.

"We'll have to spray exactly where she was when she vanished," said Dan.

"The time-spray was just inside the door," said Ally. "That must be where she dropped it when she went."

"It's lucky the walls of the shed fell outwards," said Dan. "I can see where the door was. Right by that sticky bark."

"Let me do it," said Ally. "You
might get it stuck again."

She took careful aim.

"Try to fire in short bursts," said
Dan. "Otherwise she'll come
forward from the past, shoot
straight through the present, and
disappear again into the future."

Ally pressed the trigger as lightly as she could.

What happened next was so fast, and so blurry, it was hard to see.

The air seemed to swirl. In the swirling they glimpsed the piece of sticky tree bark. It was joined by clumps of sheep fleece, tufty pieces of cotton, silkworm cocoons ... and a tiny baby.

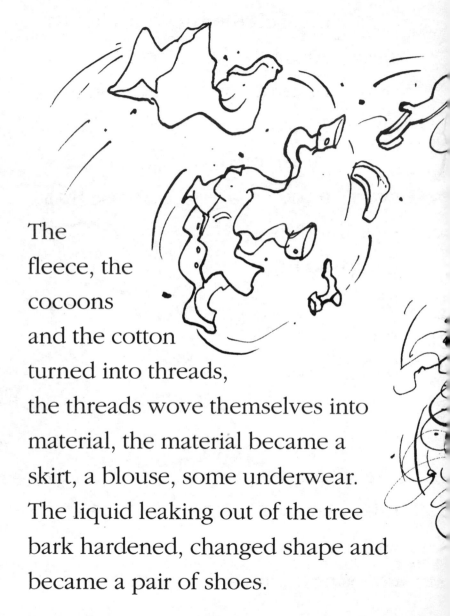

The
fleece, the
cocoons
and the cotton
turned into threads,
the threads wove themselves into
material, the material became a
skirt, a blouse, some underwear.
The liquid leaking out of the tree
bark hardened, changed shape and
became a pair of shoes.

At the same time, the baby
became a small child, an older
child, a teenager, a
young woman, a
middle-aged
woman.

Ally stopped pressing the trigger, and there in front of them was Auntie Billie, looking just as she always did, in her silk blouse, her woollen skirt and her trusty old rubber shoes.

Dan and Ally were delighted. The duck was amazed.

One second later, the time-spray overheated, backfired, shot itself into the past, and turned into several small pieces of rough, jagged rock.

"That's what metal comes from," said Dan, staring down at it.

Ally rushed forward and hugged
her aunt.

Auntie Billie hugged her back.
"Goodness," she said. "I feel quite
dizzy. My whole past life just
flashed in front of my eyes."

She looked around her and
frowned.

"Oh," she said. "I see I don't have
a shed any more. And I don't have a
table, a desk, a chair, a cushion, my
crate of files and papers or the time-
spray, either."

Then she smiled. "But I see I *do* have my box of tools and instruments, a chestnut tree, a small bamboo plantation, a smelly puddle, several interestingly shaped pieces of wood, a pile of raw cotton, and a large duck."

"I'm sorry," said Dan. "I know we shouldn't have gone into your shed."

"It's as well you did," said Auntie Billie. "I'm very glad to be back. And I'm glad the time-spray's gone. I think it was rather dangerous."

Uncle Pat came out into the garden. "I see you've been making some alterations," he said calmly. "I'm glad you've finished. The children were getting worried."

"I shall be more careful in future," said Auntie Billie.

"Do you mean you'll stop inventing?" said Uncle Pat.

"Never!" said Auntie Billie. "I'm a genius, I can't stop! But first, I think I'll build a tree-house. Much nicer than a shed don't you think?"

"We'll help you," said Dan and Ally.

"And I," said Uncle Pat,
"shall take this large duck to my
vegetable patch. It can eat the slugs
off my lettuces. It's definitely the
greatest invention yet!"

MORE WALKER SPRINTERS
For You to Enjoy

☐ 0-7445-5483-7 *The Most Brilliant Trick Ever*
by Judy Allen/Scoular Anderson   £3.50

☐ 0-7445-5499-3 *Free the Whales*
by Jamie Rix/Mike Gordon   £3.50

☐ 0-7445-5241-9 *Fort Biscuit*
by Lesley Howarth/Ann Kronheimer   £3.50

☐ 0-7445-5407-1 *Elena the Frog*
by Dyan Sheldon/Sue Heap   £3.50

☐ 0-7445-5406-3 *The Perils of Lord Reggie Parrot*
by Martin Waddell/David Parkins   £3.50

☐ 0-7445-5258-3 *Care of Henry*
by Anne Fine/Paul Howard   £3.50

☐ 0-7445-3173-X *Jolly Roger*
by Colin McNaughton   £3.50

**Walker Paperbacks are available from most booksellers,
or by post from B.B.C.S., P.O. Box 941, Hull, North Humberside HU1 3YQ**

24 hour telephone credit card line 01482 224626

To order, send: Title, author, ISBN number and price for each book ordered, your full
name and address, cheque or postal order payable to BBCS for the total amount and allow
the following for postage and packing: UK and BFPO: £1.00 for the first book, and 50p
for each additional book to a maximum of £3.50. Overseas and Eire: £2.00 for the first
book, £1.00 for the second and 50p for each additional book.

Prices and availability are subject to change without notice.

Name _____

Address _____